The Talent Contest

Creepy Crawlies

Join the Creepy Crawlies in all their
fun-packed adventures!

 Be sure to read:

Home Sweet Home

... and lots, lots more!

The Talent Contest

Tony Bradman
illustrated by Damon Burnard

SCHOLASTIC

For Chloe

Scholastic Children's Books,
Commonwealth House, 1-19 New Oxford Street,
London, WC1A 1NU, UK
a division of Scholastic Ltd
London ~ New York ~ Toronto ~ Sydney ~ Auckland
Mexico City ~ New Delhi ~ Hong Kong

First published by Scholastic Ltd, 2004

ISBN 0 439 97774 6

Printed and bound by Tien Wah Press Pte. Ltd, Singapore

10 9 8 7 6 5 4 3 2 1

Chapter One

In a corner of The Garden, beyond The
Flower Bed and underneath The Big Bush,
four little creatures were passing another
morning in their little home.

It was a day like any other.
Lucy the Ladybird
was busily tidying
up in the kitchen
after breakfast.

Billy the Beetle
was exercising
with his weights.

Imelda the Centipede was painting her
toenails, which always took ages.

And Doug the Slug … well, Doug was bored. Very, very bored.

"I'm bored, bored, bored," said Doug. "What can I do, Lucy?"

"You could play a game," said Lucy. "Or help me tidy up."

"I'm bored with playing the same old games," Doug moaned. "And tidying up is boring, too. No, I've had enough of all that. I want something … more."

"I don't understand, Doug," said Billy.
"What do you mean?"

"It's simple," Doug said dreamily, his
eyes gleaming. "I want excitement. I want
glamour. In fact, come to think of it –
I want a completely new life!"

"I'm sure I've got all kinds of talents
I've never explored," cried Doug excitedly.

"Things I could do that would take me far from here. Don't you three ever feel that way?"

"Er, no, I can't say that I do," said Billy.

"Me neither," said Lucy.

"I sometimes wish I had fewer toenails," said Imelda. "But that's about it."

Doug slumped down on the sofa. He looked very unhappy. "There's only one word for you lot," he muttered grumpily. "And that's…"

BORING!

"Calm down, Doug," said Billy. "Tell you what, let's watch TV."

"Good idea," said Lucy. "It might help you to relax, Doug."

Lucy switched on the set. A rather over-excited announcer appeared on the screen. "...Sid Snail's Talent Trail, the hottest show on Garden TV," she was saying. "Don't be shy – have a try! It could be your passport to a new life of excitement and glamour. Entry forms available from the studio..."

"Oh wow," said Doug, "that's it!"

By the time the others turned round to look at him, Doug had already gone. For a slug, Doug could move pretty fast when he had a reason to...

Chapter Two

Doug was soon back with the entry form.
He sat down at the table, got out his pencil
case, and started filling in the form while
the others looked on.

"Name?" Doug muttered to himself. "That's easy enough, Doug the Slug. Address … phone number … type of performance. What does that mean?"

"It's a talent contest, isn't it?" said Lucy. "So you have to tell them what you're actually going to do – juggle, tell jokes, dance, sing, whatever."

"I knew that," said Doug. "I was just testing you. I'm going to sing."

14

"On your own?" said Imelda. "Singers usually have a backing band."

"Do they?" said Doug. "Er … of course they do! Hey, I know. You three can be my band. How about it, guys? Please say yes! Pretty please…"

"I don't know, Doug," said Billy. "We don't have any instruments."

"No problem!" said Doug. "We can get some at The Garden Mall!"

"But we won't be able to play them," said Imelda. "We're not musicians."

"You could learn!" said Doug. "It can't be that hard, can it?"

"Well…" said Lucy at last. "I suppose we could have a go. We are friends, after all, and if this is what Doug wants to do, then we should help him."

Billy and Imelda both shrugged and smiled, and it was settled.

"Fantastic!" yelled Doug. "Come on, everybody – follow me!"

They set off for The Garden Mall.

When they got there they went to Gary the Hopper's Hip-Hop Shop, and looked at the instruments. They were very expensive, but Gary was cool, and said he'd take them back if things didn't work out. So they bought a drum set and a couple of guitars. Lucy paid.

"Right, let's go home," said Lucy. "I think we should practise."

"Plenty of time for that!" said Doug. "I have to deliver my entry form."

Doug hurried off, and the others followed, carrying the instruments.

But there was a huge crowd at the studio gates, a horde of little creatures pushing and shoving and getting cross and shouting. They were all trying to deliver their entry forms at the same time.

"Oh no!" Doug moaned in despair. "I'll never get my entry form in!"

"Oh yes you will," someone said in a smooth, silky voice. They turned round and saw a large spider in a flashy suit. "With my help, that is…"

Chapter Three

"Allow me to introduce myself," the spider drawled. He scurried over and put a long, spiky leg round Doug's shoulders. "Spence the Spider is the name, taking care of talent is my game. And you look like a very talented young slug to me, son. It also looks like you badly need a manager."

"I don't think he does," Lucy said quickly. "Come on, Doug."

"Hang on a second, Lucy," Doug murmured. "I want to hear what he has to say. What do you mean, Mr Spider? What exactly could you do for me?"

"Call me Spence," said the spider with a big smile. "Well, for starters I could make sure your entry form gets into the studio. Hand it over."

Doug
did as he
was told.

Spence took the form, scuttled up a
nearby bush, then lowered himself beyond
the studio fence.

A minute later he was back.

"There you go," said Spence. "Job done. You're in the show, son."

"Wow!" said Doug. "Terrific! You can definitely be my manager!"

"Oh, Doug!" said Lucy. "Perhaps you ought to think about it a bit…"

But it was too late. Spence had already whipped a wodge of papers out of a pocket. "OK, sign here," he said, "and here … here … and here. Right, now you and I need to have a little chat, er … what did you say your name was?"

"Doug the Slug," said Doug as Spence steered him away from his friends.

"Really?" Spence said quietly. "Umm ... we might have to change that." Spence took a crafty look over his shoulder at Lucy, Billy and Imelda. "And a few other things, too," he added. "Are those three your backing band?"

"Er ... yes, they are," said Doug. "I haven't thought of a band name yet."

"I wouldn't bother, son," said Spence. "You'll have to ditch them."

"I can't do that!" said Doug. "They're my friends!"

"Listen," said Spence. "Do you want to win this contest or not?" Doug nodded. "Well, you won't with that lot as your backing band."

"But what shall I say to them?" said Doug.

"You leave that to me," said Spence. "I'll take care of it. That's what a manager's for, after all. Then I'll see about getting you a hot new band."

Spence scuttled off towards Doug's friends, with Doug trailing after him.

"I'm doing the right thing," Doug muttered.

I think I am, anyway...

Chapter Four

Lucy, Billy and Imelda were surprised when Spence said they were being sacked. But they didn't argue, as Doug seemed to agree with him.

Even so, they were all rather worried about their friend.

"Are you sure you're going to be okay, Doug?" Billy asked.

"He'll be fine," Spence said before Doug had a chance to reply. "Now come on, we've got work to do."

Spence scuttled off, and Doug followed.

He took a last look at his friends, and they waved until they couldn't see him any more.

Then they sadly went home, stopping on the way to return the instruments to Gary, who gave Lucy her money back.

Well, most of it, anyway.

Meanwhile, Spence led Doug to a part of
The Garden he'd never been in before.

They went into a dark, crowded, smelly bar, and Spence led Doug over to a table. Sitting round it was the meanest, nastiest, ugliest-looking bunch of cockroaches Doug had ever seen. They stared at him, and Doug gulped.

"Meet your new band, son," said Spence. "I've found us a singer, boys!"

"He'd better be good," growled the biggest cockroach. "For your sake."

"Yeah, we want to win!" growled the others. "Win, win, win, win…"

"Don't worry about them," said Spence. "They're nice lads, really, er… deep down. Anyway, let's go and sort out some new clothes for you."

A little while later Doug was back at the studio with Spence and his new backing band. And now he wasn't Doug any more. He was Ronnie, lead singer of Ronnie and the Roaches. Sid Snail, however, wasn't impressed.

"Not another singer in shades and a leather jacket," he moaned. "And haven't I seen this band before? Aren't they the lot who get into fights?"

"No, Sid," said Spence.
"Cross my heart.
Whatever gave
you that idea?"

"You don't have a heart, Spence," said
Sid. "Oh well, maybe a fight will be good
for the ratings. Okay, you and the roaches
are on last, kid."

Doug waited with the other performers, who were pushing and shoving and getting cross. He peeked at the judges, who looked very fierce. And the creatures in the audience weren't very friendly, either. They were shouting and booing and throwing things.

Suddenly Doug felt scared and lonely and a long way from home.

Chapter Five

Meanwhile, back in the little house, Lucy, Billy and Imelda were sitting round the TV set. They were all feeling very nervous for their friend.

"I can't bear it!" said Imelda, peering from behind a cushion.

"Hush now, it's starting!" said Lucy, and they leaned forward...

Back at the studio Doug watched the other performers do their stuff. His own nerves were getting worse by the second. It didn't help that the crowd booed everyone off before they could even finish.

The judges said horrible things about each act, too.

Finally it was time for Ronnie and the Roaches to perform.

"Take it away, boys!" said Sid.

But they were. Or at least, Doug was. The Roaches went straight into a song Doug knew, *Rock Around The Garden*. Doug opened his mouth to sing the words … and what came out was a terrible, awful, unbelievable noise.

"Boo!" yelled the crowd. "Get off! You can't sing for toffee! Boo!"

Doug shut his mouth. It was true, he realized. He couldn't sing … but it didn't matter. He didn't want to be a singer. He didn't want excitement or glamour any more, or a new life.

He just wanted to be with his friends.

"HELP!" wailed Spence and Sid as they disappeared under a heap of extremely angry creatures. The Roaches weren't very happy about losing yet again. And the audience hadn't enjoyed the show much either.

But Doug had already gone. As we know, for a slug he could move pretty fast... In fact, he made sure he got home as quickly as he could.

"Oh hi, Doug," said Lucy when he arrived.
"You're just in time for supper. How did
things go at the talent contest? We didn't
watch it, did we?"

"Er, no, we didn't," said Billy.
"We were, er … far too busy," said Imelda.

"Well, I lost," said Doug. "So I'm afraid you're stuck with me."

"That's OK," said Lucy, smiling. "We like it that way."

And Doug liked it that way too.